MW01041475

SHAMLANDERS

WRITTEN BY

Betty Paraskevas

ILLUSTRATED BY

Michael Paraskevas

HARCOURT BRACE & COMPANY

San Diego   New York   London

Requests for permission to make copies of any
part of the work should be mailed to: Permissions
Department, Harcourt Brace & Company,
8th Floor, Orlando, Florida 32887.

Library of Congress Cataloging-in-Publication Data
Paraskevas, Betty.
Shamlanders/Betty Paraskevas; illustrated by
Michael Paraskevas. — 1st ed.
p.   cm.
Summary: A child wanders through a strange desertscape
inhabited by Shamlanders, polka-dot beasts, and argyle
sheep, among other fantastic beings, until he is transported
via a bouquet of glowing balloons to his own bed.
ISBN 0-15-292854-5
[1. Imagination — Fiction. 2. Animals, Mythical — Fiction.
3. Stories in rhyme.] I. Paraskevas, Michael, 1961–   ill.
II. Title.
PZ8.3.P162Sh   1993
[Fic] — dc20   92-32980

First edition
A B C D E

The illustrations in this book were done in gouache
and acrylics on Strathmore 100% rag paper.
The text type was set in Cochin by
Thompson Type, San Diego, California.
The display type was set in Eastman by
Harcourt Brace & Company Photocomposition
Center, San Diego, California.
Color separations by Bright Arts, Ltd., Singapore
Printed and bound by Tien Wah Press, Singapore
Production supervision by Warren Wallerstein
and Kent MacElwee
Designed by Michael Farmer

Printed in Singapore

To Ned Dougherty, Ginnie Kearns, and Michael Christopher
— B. P. and M. P.

I was walking down a road that led out of town.
I had to cross a bridge but the gate was down.
A cranky old man held out his hand.
"It's ten cents to get to Nowhere Land."
"Is that the place where the sky is always blue?"
"If you're looking for blue skies, Nowhere Land's for you."
I gave him a dime and I had to wait
While the cranky old man cranked up the gate.

I stepped off the bridge on the other side,
Landed in sand, and began to slide
Down the edge of a dune. Nowhere Land
Was nothing but a big, hot desert of sand.
Something seemed to move, or could it be
My eyes were playing tricks on me?
I realized the bridge I'd crossed
Had disappeared. And I knew I was lost.

A ferocious beast with a polka-dot hide
Came up and asked if I'd like a ride.
The sand in my shoes made my feet feel like lead.
"How much will it cost me to ride?" I said.
"One dollar more than you've got," he replied.
"Well, why did you offer to give me a ride,
Then ask for more than you knew I could pay?"
"I'm not really sure," he said with a grin, "I guess I'm just funny that way."

"Nonsense," I said, and since I had no ride
I walked away, but the ferocious beast cried,
"Don't leave me alone. What will I do?
Wherever you're going, I'm going, too."
In the shadow of a cactus taller than a tree,
I sat down to rest, and the beast sat next to me.
Coming toward us quickly from the east,
I saw a second ferocious beast.
The first beast whispered, "I hope he moves along.
I don't think I like him, his spots are all wrong."
But the second beast stopped — "Unfortunate fellow!
Your polka dots are red. They should be yellow."

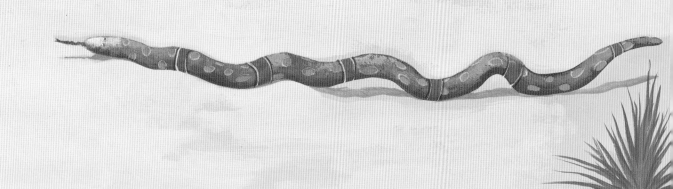

"If my polka dots were yellow," the first beast replied,
"I'd look like you and I'd have to hide."
There I was in the middle of a fight
With a beast on my left and a beast on my right.
To distract them I asked how they got to this place.
A grin spread over the first beast's face,
"I can't be sure, but I'm inclined
To believe that we came from the back of your mind."

We walked till we came to a little red stand
Where shovels and pails for digging in the sand
Were sold by a man in a three-piece suit
Who was playing a tune on a little tin flute.
He asked if I'd buy a shovel and pail,
Because up until then he had not made a sale.
I said I was sorry but in a desert so big
The last thing I wanted to do was dig.
So the elegant gentleman shrugged and then
Played on his little tin flute again.

The beast on my left and the beast on my right
Set my nerves on edge. They continued to fight.
If the first beast said yes, the second beast said no.
If the first one walked fast, the second one walked slow.
A man with a bullhorn was directing a crew,
In his knickers and knee socks and pith helmet, too.
They were making a film, he stopped to explain,
And there'd been a delay while they waited for rain.

We next came upon a herd of argyle sheep
With their shepherd on the sand, fast asleep.
The ferocious beasts had never seen
Argyle sheep and they turned envy green.
The shepherd leapt up, a bit perturbed
Because his nap had been disturbed,
But he laughed when I mentioned there might be
Something on the desert, watching me.
"There's only the Shamlanders, and since you're a stranger,
They think you're a threat — but you're in no danger.
There are many Shamlanders in Nowhere Land,
Living in houses they build on the sand.
They keep to themselves; they like it that way.
The desert is perfect for the games they play.
And every night there's a place they go.
It's somewhere out there. It's the Stucco Chateau."

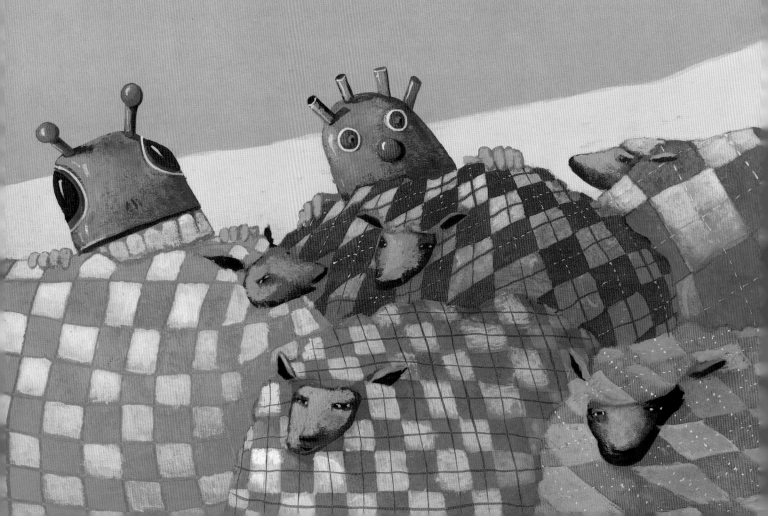

Suddenly a windstorm hurled the sand around.
I saw red and yellow spots as I fell to the ground.
And when it was over, how the beasts carried on.
They wouldn't stop crying; their polka dots were gone.

I saw a man painting the desert and I asked if he might spare
A little red, a little yellow. He agreed, and with great care
I painted back their polka dots. The beasts were good as new.
The man watched us hurry away; I felt the Shamlanders watching us, too.

We moved in closer; the beasts were in a trance.
Bewitched by the tango, they both began to dance.
It was most peculiar to finally be
Watching the Shamlanders who'd been watching me.

Then up came a doorman, holding a bouquet
Of glowing white balloons, and chased us away.
"You can't come in." His voice was gruff.
"No strangers allowed; you're not FAAAAAABULOUS ENOUGH!"
"But all I want to do is get away from this place."
He paused for a moment and studied my face.
"There's only one way out of Nowhere Land.
You must rise above it." Then he placed in my hand
The strings that held the glowing bouquet
Of white balloons. I began to sway.

My feet left the ground. I was up in the night,
Looking down on the beasts, holding on tight.
"Good-bye," I called to the beasts below,
"I'm sorry to leave you behind."
"Don't worry about us — we'll see you again;
We came from the back of your mind."

The balloons and I continued to climb
For what seemed to be a very long time,
Leaving Shamlanders, dreamers, and fools behind,
As well as the beasts from the back of my mind.
I landed so hard on the top of my bed
That I could see polka dots, yellow and red.
Memories like photographs with time will fade,
But Nowhere Land has always stayed
In the back of my mind, and now and then
I see a familiar face again.